Everybody Loves Butterflies

Written by Tanis Taylor
Illustrated by Masumi Furukawa

PaRragon

Bath • New York • Singapore • Hong Kong • Cologne • Delhi
Melbourne • Amsterdam • Johannesburg • Shenzhen

To Jess,
Who always
loves just where
she is.

T.T.

For
Yasushi
& Ryo

M.F.

This edition published by Parragon
Books Ltd in 2013

Parragon Books Ltd
Chartist House
15–17 Trim Street
Bath BA1 1HA, UK
www.parragon.com

Published by arrangement with
Meadowside Children's Books

Text © Tanis Taylor 2013
Illustrations © Masumi
Furukawa 2013

ISBN 978-1-4723-3180-9

Printed in China

Little Caterpillar didn't like change.
His brothers and sisters had all turned into butterflies
and he knew that one day he would too.

But he wanted to stay
a caterpillar forever.

"Change is good!"
said a lovely swan.

"Don't you want to become
a beautiful butterfly?"

But Little Caterpillar didn't.
"I *like* being a caterpillar.
I don't **ever** want to change!"

"Caterpillars are so dull,"
said a bright dragonfly.

"Butterflies are all the
colours of the rainbow."

But Little Caterpillar
thought that so many
colours would only
make him dizzy.

"You will eat nectar from flowers," said a buzzy bumblebee.

"Nectar is deeelicious!"

But Little Caterpillar liked eating leaves.
He liked the satisfying crunch they made.

"Think of all the adventures you'll have!"
said a tiny ant.

"You'll see the world!"

But Little Caterpillar
didn't see the point.
He was happy here.

"What about flying?"
asked a friendly robin.

"Butterflies can fly high in the sky!"
Little Caterpillar looked up. The sky seemed
an awfully long way away.

"Everybody loves butterflies,"
said a spindly spider.

"Who do you know who
loves caterpillars?"

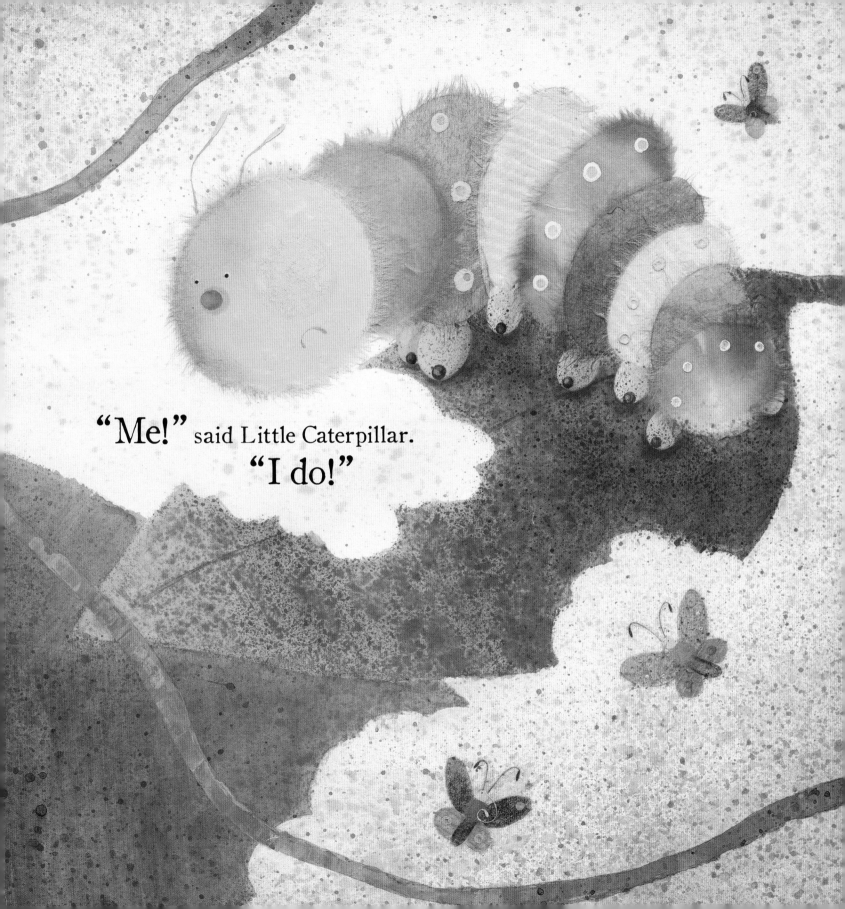

"Me!" said Little Caterpillar.
"I do!"

Little Caterpillar went to see Owl.
Owl was the oldest and the wisest
animal he knew.

"Oh, Owl.
Must I become a butterfly?
Why can't I stay a caterpillar for ever and ever?"

"Little Caterpillar," smiled the owl. "You are a caterpillar now and one day you will be a butterfly. You will still be you. **You will just be you with wings!"**

That very night, Little Caterpillar
snuggled down deep and had
a long, long sleep.

And when he woke up...

...he had wings! Glorious wings!
Wings with red and purple spots.
He flapped them a few times to dry.

Amazing!

He ate nectar
from the flowers...

He flew up high in the sky.
He looked down at the world.

and flew a loop-the-loop!
Fantastic!

"Yippee!" he whooped, as he whizzed past Owl's tree. "I love being a butterfly! I want to be a butterfly for ever and ever!"

Old Owl laughed. "I'm glad to see that some things don't change!"

And Little Butterfly
wheeled through the sky
on his brand new wings,
waving to all his friends.

1. Larva

A butterfly starts life as an egg. The female will lay her eggs on a juicy leaf and when the larvae (baby caterpillars) hatch they will eat their way out!

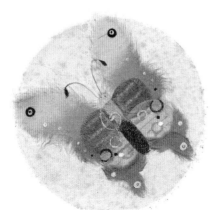

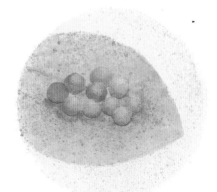

The Amazing Life Cycle of a Butterfly

2. Caterpillar

Caterpillars are born hungry. All they do is eat and grow! When they are ready they find a safe spot and attach themselves to a leaf with some sticky gloop. This hardens and is called a 'chrysalis'.

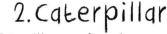

5. Adult Butterfly

There are more than 20,000 types of butterflies in the world. There are ones as big as a bird and tiny ones the size of a coin, speedy ones (who can fly up to 12 mph) and lazy ones. Over their lifetime, they will feed, find a mate, lay their own eggs, and so start the amazing cycle all over again.

4. Butterfly

Weeks or even months later, the butterfly breaks out of its chrysalis. It pumps blood into its wet wings and lets its new body harden in the sun. Within hours it is ready to fly.

3. Chrysalis

The caterpillar – now called a 'pupa' – hangs in its chrysalis. Inside, the most amazing changes are taking place – the caterpillar's body is breaking itself down using the same juices it used to digest its food. Some things stay the same, others are totally new – like wings!